DOG BREATH

THE HORRIBLE TROUBLE WITH HALLY TOSIS

DAV PILKEY

SCHOLASTIC INC. • NEW YORK

For Mom and Dad and Halle

Library of Congress Cataloging-in-Publication Data available

ISBN 978-1-338-53923-3

10 9 8 7 6 5 4 3 2 1   19 20 21 22 23

Printed in Malaysia   108
This edition first printing, October 2019

Book design by Dav Pilkey and Kathleen Westray

The illustrations in this book were made using acrylics,
watercolors, pencils, Magic Markers, and Dijon mustard.

There once was a dog named Hally,
who lived with the Tosis family.
Hally Tosis was a very good dog,
but she had a big problem.

Hally Tosis had horrible breath.
Whenever Hally Tosis opened her mouth,
horrible things happened.

When the children took Hally Tosis
for a walk, everyone else walked

on the other side of the street.
Even skunks avoided Hally Tosis.

But the real trouble started one day
when Grandma Tosis stopped by
for a cup of tea...

. . . and Hally jumped up to say hello.

Mr. and Mrs. Tosis were not amused. "Something has to be done about that smelly dog," they said.

The next day, Mr. and Mrs. Tosis
decided to find a new home for Hally.

The children knew that the only way
they could save their dog was to get
rid of her bad breath. So they took
Hally Tosis to the top of a mountain
that had a breathtaking view.

They hoped that the breathtaking view would take Hally's breath away...

...but it didn't.

Next, the children took Hally Tosis
to a very exciting movie.

They hoped that all the excitement
would leave Hally breathless...

. . . but it didn't.

Finally, the children took Hally Tosis to a carnival. They hoped that Hally would lose her breath on the speedy roller coaster...

YOU'LL LOSE YOUR BREATH ON OUR ROLLERCOASTER

Mmmm!
HOT-DOGS!

FREE BALLOON

...but that idea stunk, too!

The plans to change Hally's bad
breath had failed. Now, only a
miracle could save Hally Tosis.
Sadly, the three friends said
good-night, unaware that a
miracle was just on the horizon.

Later that night, when everyone was
sound asleep, two sneaky burglars
crept into the Tosis house.
The two burglars were tiptoeing through
the dark quiet rooms when suddenly
they came upon Hally Tosis.

"Yikes," whispered one burglar. "It's a big, mean, scary dog!"

"Aw, don't be silly," whispered the other burglar. "That's only a cute, little, fuzzy puppy!"

The two burglars giggled at the sight
of such a friendly little dog.
"That dog couldn't hurt a fly,"
whispered one burglar.
"Come here, poochie poochie!"
whispered the other.
So Hally Tosis came over and gave
the burglars a nice big kiss.

The next morning, the Tosis family awoke to find two burglars passed out cold on their living room floor.

It was a miracle!

The Tosis family got a big reward
for turning in the crooks, and soon
Hally Tosis was the most famous
crime-fighting dog in the country.

In the end, Mr. and Mrs. Tosis changed their minds about finding a new home for Hally. They decided to keep their wonderful watchdog after all.

Because life without Hally Tosis
just wouldn't make any *scents!*